England

New
Jersey

N

Atlantic
Ocean

To Judith Whipple

Rings on her fingers . . . — J. S.

For Sue — C. S.

Text copyright © 2002 by Joseph Slate
Illustrations copyright © 2002 by Craig Spearing
All rights reserved.
Marshall Cavendish, 99 White Plains Road, Tarrytown, NY 10591
www.marshallcavendish.com

Library of Congress Cataloging-in-Publication Data
Slate, Joseph.
The great big wagon that rang: how the Liberty Bell was saved / by Joseph Slate ;
illustrations by Craig Spearing.
p.   cm.
Summary: A farmer rescues the Liberty Bell from the British in his big wagon.
ISBN 0-7614-5108-0
[1. Liberty Bell—Fiction. 2. Wagons—Fiction.]   I. Spearing, Craig, ill. II. Title.
PZ7.S6289 Gr 2002   [E]—dc21   2002000835

The text of this book is set in 15 point Palatino.
Printed in Malaysia

First edition

1 3 5 6 4 2

The Great Big Wagon That Rang

·How the Liberty Bell Was Saved·

·Written by·
Joseph Slate

·Illustrated by·
Craig Spearing

Marshall Cavendish · New York

The woodsman's ax rang
like a struck bell.

It felled the hickory and oak
that boxed the bed
and spoked the wheels
of the great big wagon.

The blacksmith's hammer clanged
like a great bell.

It shaped the iron
that shod the wheels
that rolled the bed
of the great big wagon.

The farmer filled
the wagon with hay
to settle his pumpkins.

He hung his four horses
with lattenbells that jingled.

He then set off
with a "Git" and a "Hey!
We're on our way
to Philadel-phi-a!"

In Union Square
the farmer ring-a-linged
a market bell.

"Buy my pumpkins, pelts of foxes,
honey and brooms
and apple boxes
that sit in the bed
of this great big wagon."

By the end of the day,
the farmer had sold
all his goods except the hay.

He fed some of the hay
to his horses—
but not all.

His horses knew
it was time to go.
They shook their lattenbells.
"Jing-a-ling,
hear us ring.
We're going home,
we're going home,
with a bed of hay
boxed by the boards
that roll on the wheels
of our great big wagon."

"But whoa," said the farmer,
"we cannot go."
For over their heads
soldiers lowered a giant bell.

It dinged and donged
and hung in the way
of the great big wagon.

"The redcoats are coming,"
a soldier cried.
"To take this bell
to melt it down
to make the shot
to fill their guns
and tie our hands
to their mad old King."

"Lower it here,"
the farmer said,
"into my sturdy wagon."

They rolled in the dark
over rutty roads,
near the redcoats' camp,
with the giant bell
hidden in the straw
of the great big wagon.

But the horses' bells
went jing-a-ling,
and two Redcoats
stood to see this thing
boxed by the boards
of the great big wagon.

"Check if you must,"
  the farmer said,
"but it's only hay
  and empty boxes—
  all that's left
  of my market day."

And the redcoats said,
"Get! Get on your way."

And off he went
with a clink and a clack,
the great big bell
on the wagon's back
to the church of Zion,
and they hid it away
'till the redcoats fled
Philadel-phi-a.

And this is the bell,
the Liberty Bell—
    oh, now you can see
    by the dawn's early light
—was hauled right back
and rang for joy
that we were free,
rang high and low
for the great big wagon
that made it so.

Author's note

Behind the story of the Liberty Bell is the story of the covered wagon, the Conestoga. In about 1750 German immigrants in Pennsylvania's Conestoga Valley began building them. Sturdy wagons were needed to carry their produce to Philadelphia markets and shipping ports. Conestogas were a great improvement over the wagons then in use in colonial America. They could carry tons of goods. A curved floor impeded load shifting. High broad wheels lifted and steadied the carriage over rutty roads. Later, smaller Conestogas—the prairie schooners—wheeled our pioneers west.

A Conestoga most probably carried the Liberty Bell. But there is uncertainty over who drove the wagon on that legendary night in September 1777. Frederick Leaser, John Jacob Mickley, and others have all been credited with hauling the Liberty Bell. Adding to the confusion was the number of bells. Between eleven and thirteen were removed from two churches and the state house in Philadelphia. The combined weight was about 13,000 pounds. At least three wagons were needed to carry the bells. Mishaps occurred along the way. As historian John Baer Stoudt has written, "There [were] enough large bells, enough wagons, and surely there is enough glory to go around."

Acknowledgments

I am indebted to Joseph R. Johnson, a librarian at the Free Library of Philadelphia, for directing me to various historical documents and sources, among these the Reverend John Baer Stoudt's 1928 address, *Frederick Leaser and the Hauling of the Liberty Bell*. For those interested in colonial wagons, Edwin Tunis's *Colonial Craftsmen and the Beginning of American Industry* with his finely detailed illustrations, published by Johns Hopkins University Press, is very useful. In keeping with what has become a legend in American history, I have taken liberties with the story. It seemed to have its own poetry, and so I made it into a song that would ring out to children, where a simple telling might not.

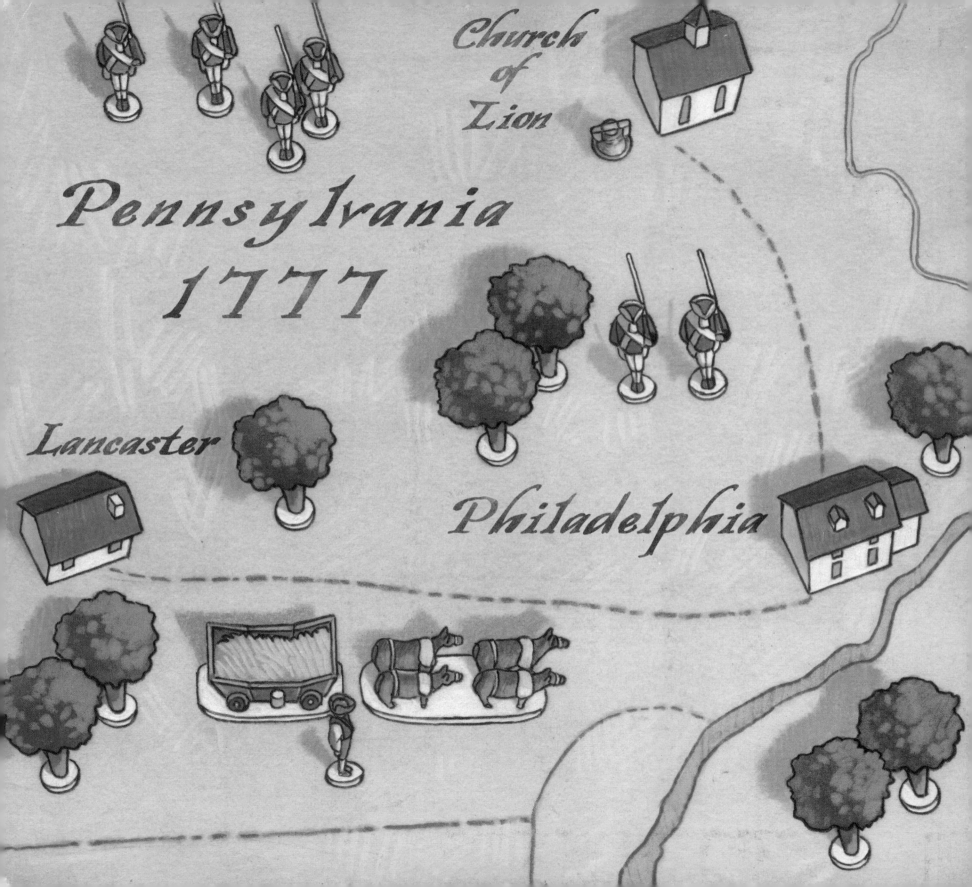